SPARKY AND SPIKE

Margot E. Kelman
Illustrated by Jean Ashton

SOUND **S**YSTEM **S**TORIES

Sound System Stories™ target specific sounds or sound combinations using syntactically and semantically appropriate text.

Read with Me!™ Strategies for *Sparky and Spike*
Echo Reading ~ Paired Reading ~ Friendly Questions

/sp/ blends

Sparky and Spike
By Margot E. Kelman, Ph.D., CCC-SLP

Illustrated by Jean Ashton
Colorized by Melissa Cornwell

Sound System Stories Logo by Melissa Cornwell

ISBN-13   978-0-9968945-0-0

Layout by Shari Robertson and Melissa Cornwell

Printed in the United States of America

READ WITH ME PRESS
www.readwme.com

A division of:
Dynamic Resources, LLC
5306 Tanoma Road
Indiana, PA 15701
www.dynamic-resources.org

To my inspirational phonology mentors, Mary Louise Edwards and Barbara Hodson, with gratitude.

~Margot Kelman

To Tori Jean. When you were born your mother, Vanessa, and I became instantly obsolete. What is true for a good book is also true for children; the job of leaving the world in better shape than you found it is now yours. Great job so far, kiddo.

~Your Godmother, Jean

Sparky and Spike are spiders.

Sparky is yellow and has orange spots.

Spike is purple and has no spots.

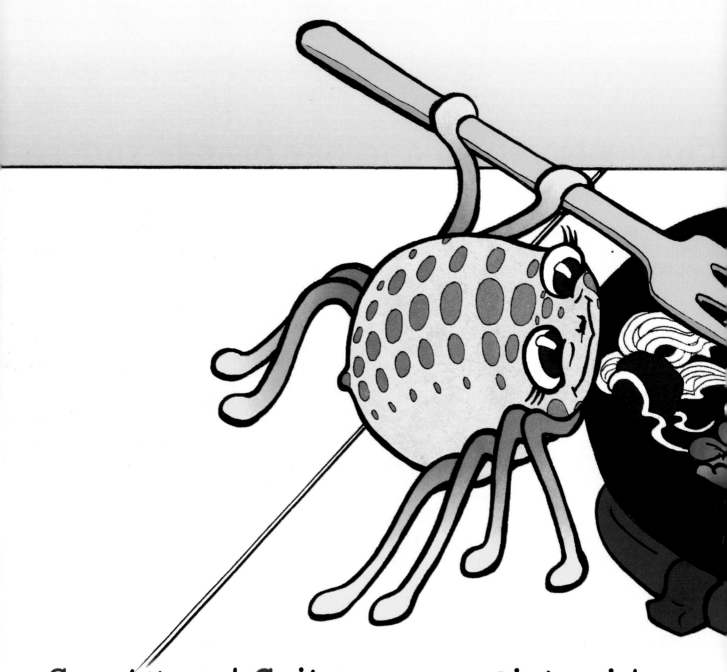

Sparky and Spike are special spiders.

They can COOK!

Sometimes, they spill things.

They use a spoon or a sponge
to clean up.

Sparky likes to eat spicy spaghetti.

Spike likes to eat spicy spinach.

Spicy Spinach?

That does not sound tasty, but Spike likes it!

Spicy spaghetti!

Spicy spinach!

Maybe Sparky and Spike car

cook for you some day!

THE END

About the Author

Margot E. Kelman, Ph.D., CCC-SLP has over 30 years of experience as a speech-language pathologist in the schools, in private practice, and as Speech-Language Clinic Director at Syracuse University.

Margot co-authored, with Mary Louise Edwards, *Phonogroup: A Practical Guide for Enhancing Phonological Remediation* and contributed a chapter, 'Acquisition of Speech Sounds and Phonological Patterns' in Barbara Hodson's text, *Evaluation and Enhancing Children's Phonological Systems.*

Her interests are in early childhood speech, language, and literacy development. She loves helping young children learn and grow!

About the Illustrator

Jean Ashton is an artist and filmmaker from Farmington, Michigan. Jean has spent her life honing her creative abilities. She earned her B.A. in Film Arts with an emphasis in Arts and Creative Writing at California State University, Long Beach, one of the top ten film schools in the nation. Jean also holds a degree in commercial design.

"A picture is worth a thousand words" is the premise that has, and always will, drive her creative life of writing, digital media, visual arts, and illustration.

Visit www.ashtonality.com to find more information about Jean as well as her "How To" creative series, her children's sleep DVD, *Fuzzy Warm Sleepy Dorm*, and comedic film reviews.

How to Use this Book

Sparky and Spike is designed to help children learn to produce /sp/ combinations in conversational contexts.

Here's how you can help your child build key speech, language, and literacy skills and a life-long love of reading.

◇◇◇

❏ Read the story aloud, emphasizing the target sounds in words.

❏ Once the child is familiar with the story, encourage him or her to fill in the target words using pausing and intonation cues.

❏ Use the included flashcards to review the vocabulary and retell the story.

❏ Play memory using pairs of each word card. Word cards can be photocopied or downloaded at www.dynamic-resources.org or readwme.com.

❏ Encourage the child to make up a sentence using a single card or a whole new story using as many of the cards as he or she likes.

❏ Act out the story using the stick puppets included.

❏ Ask questions about the characters in the story and have the child hold up the puppet or flashcard that answers the question. (**Adult:** *Who likes spinach?* **Child:** *Spike!* **Adult:** *What does Sparky like to eat?* **Child:** *Spaghetti!*)

❏ Most importantly, laugh and have fun with Sparky and Spike!